ROSIE

Based on *The Railway Series* by the Rev. W. Awdry

Illustrations by

Robin Davies and Phil Jacobs

EGMONT

3
5
Annie

EGMONT

We bring stories to life

First published in Great Britain 2007
by Egmont UK Limited
239 Kensington High Street, London W8 6SA

ISBN 978 1 4052 3150 3
1 3 5 7 9 10 8 6 4 2
Printed in Great Britain

The Forest Stewardship Council (FSC) is an international, non-governmental organisation dedicated to promoting responsible management of the world's forests. FSC operates a system of forest certification and product labelling that allows consumers to identify wood and wood-based products from well managed forests.

For more information about Egmont's paper buying policy please visit www.egmont.co.uk/ethicalpublishing

For more information about the FSC please visit their website at www.fsc.uk.org

TO THE TRAINS →

This is a story about Rosie, a chirpy tank engine who liked to copy Thomas. This made Thomas cross, until one day, Rosie proved just how Useful she could be . . .

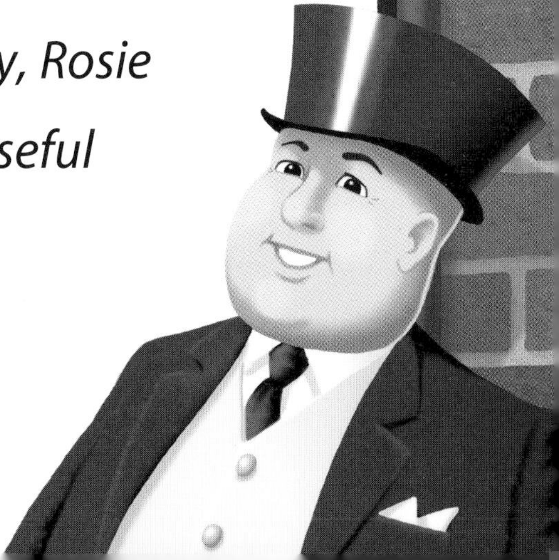

It was the stormy season on the Island of Sodor and Thomas was busy delivering mail to a far part of the Island.

At the end of the line, on a farm at the top of the high hill, lived a little girl called Alice. Today was Alice's birthday and Thomas was going to deliver all her birthday cards and presents.

While Thomas was at the station being loaded up, Rosie, a little, purple tank engine, pulled up beside him.

"Hello, Thomas," puffed Rosie. Her puff was almost exactly like Thomas'.

Rosie tried to do everything just like Thomas. She tried to wheesh like him and she tried to whistle like him. She liked Thomas so much that she wanted to be just like him.

Thomas didn't like this. It made him cross.

"Where are you going?" asked Rosie.

"It's Alice's birthday," replied Thomas. "I'm taking all her presents to High Farm. I'm going to make sure she gets them all on time."

Just then Harold swooped down. "I'm afraid I've got a storm warning," he whirred. "You had better be careful on those high tracks, Thomas, the winds can cause landslides up there."

ROLD
1

Thomas didn't want to let Alice down.

"High winds don't bother me," he puffed.

"Or me!" puffed Rosie. "I'll come as your back engine."

But Thomas didn't want Rosie to come. "No thank you. I'll manage on my own," he chuffed and pulled away quickly.

But Rosie wouldn't take no for an answer. She cheekily followed after him.

1

Thomas sped along the line to High Farm. His engine was working very hard.

The sky grew darker and darker and soon it was pouring with rain.

"Rosie can't follow me now," thought Thomas. "She isn't strong enough."

But Thomas was wrong. Rosie was following right behind. She whistled cheerfully.

Thomas was very annoyed.

When he came to the next junction Thomas could either take the longer, easier track to High Farm, or the shorter and harder track.

Thomas knew the longer way was safer. Especially in such stormy weather.

"I'll take the shorter way," he wheeshed. "Then Rosie won't follow me."

Thomas puffed furiously up the steep track, as the storm grew stronger and stronger. Thomas was sure Rosie couldn't be behind him now.

All of a sudden there was a loud crack! Stones tumbled down the bank in front of Thomas. They covered the track completely. Thomas couldn't go forward.

"Cinders and ashes!" he cried.

What was Thomas going to do now? He still wanted to deliver Alice's presents but the track was blocked.

"I'll just have to bash my way through," thought Thomas.

Soon, Thomas was up to his buffers in mud and stones. He tried to push on but he couldn't. He tried to back out but he couldn't.

Thomas was stuck!

"Peep, peep!" another engine was coming up the track. It was Rosie!

Thomas felt very silly, but he was very glad to see Rosie.

"I'll go and get help," she chuffed.

"Wait," puffed Thomas. "Please will you deliver Alice's presents for me?"

Rosie was very happy that Thomas had asked her to deliver Alice's presents.

"Of course I will," she chuffed happily.

Rosie was soon coupled up to Thomas' trucks. She pulled away and steamed back to the longer, safer track to High Farm.

Thomas waited for Rosie to come back. He was very happy Rosie had followed him, after all.

Sodor Mail

Very soon, Rosie came puffing back down the line. "Alice's mother has telephoned for help," she told Thomas. "Edward is coming to pull you out."

Then Thomas noticed that Rosie had a passenger on board. It was Alice!

"Thank you for making sure I got my presents," Alice told Thomas. "They were very nice."

"I couldn't have done it without Rosie's help," chuffed Thomas, truthfully. "Now we can all celebrate your birthday together!"

Thomas peeped, happily.

Rosie peeped, too. Just like Thomas.

Sodor
Mail

3
5
Annie

The Thomas Story Library is THE definitive collection of stories about Thomas and ALL his friends.

There are now 50 stories from the Island of Sodor to collect!

So go on, start your Thomas Story Library NOW!

A Fantastic Offer for Thomas the Tank Engine Fans!

STICK POUND COIN HERE

In every Thomas Story Library book like this one, you will find a special token. Collect 6 Thomas tokens and we will send you a brilliant Thomas poster, and a double-sided bedroom door hanger! Simply tape a £1 coin in the space above, and fill out the form overleaf.

Cut along the dotted line

TO BE COMPLETED BY AN ADULT

To apply for this great offer, ask an adult to complete the coupon below and send it with a pound coin and 6 tokens, to:
THOMAS OFFERS, PO BOX 715, HORSHAM RH12 5WG

 Please send a Thomas poster and door hanger. I enclose 6 tokens plus a £1 coin. (Price includes P&P)

Fan's name..

Address..

....Postcode..............................

Date of birth..

Name of parent/guardian..

Signature of parent/guardian..

Please allow 28 days for delivery. Offer is only available while stocks last. We reserve the right to change the terms of this offer at any time and we offer a 14 day money back guarantee. This does not affect your statutory rights.

 Data Protection Act: If you do not wish to receive other similar offers from us or companies we recommend, please tick this box. Offers apply to UK only.

Cut along the dotted line